ALL THE YEAR ROUND

To our good friend Klaus

First published in 2017 by Andersen Press Ltd., 20 Vauxhall Bridge Road, London SW1V 2SA.

Text copyright © John Yeoman, 2017. Illustration copyright © Quentin Blake, 2017.

First edition.

Printed and bound in Malaysia.

British Library Cataloguing in Publication Data available.

ISBN 978 1 78344 613 1

ALL THE YEAR ROUND

words by John Yeoman

pictures by Quentin Blake

ANDERSEN PRESS

SPRING   SUMMER   AUTUMN   WINTER

There are hundreds of reasons
For welcoming seasons!

JANUARY

"You should wear a thicker sweater." "Take your woolly scarf: it's cold."
Why not put your fur-lined boots on?" Do they think I'm five years old?

I would be a great deal happier if I weren't obliged to wear
All those extra layers like an insulated polar bear.

Wouldn't it be fun to go out, just for once, dressed as I please:

Plastic flip-flops, baggy t-shirt, jeans cut off above the knees.

FEBRUARY

Now and then I get up extra-early, just to make
A super-scrumptious yummy-yummy, light-as-air-type cake.
I weigh and mix and stir and knead, till everything's just so;
The kitchen air is fragrant with the sweetly-smelling dough.

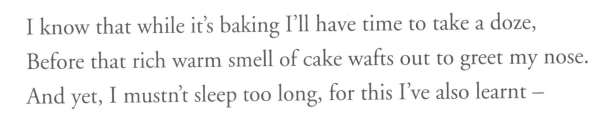

I know that while it's baking I'll have time to take a doze,
Before that rich warm smell of cake wafts out to greet my nose.
And yet, I mustn't sleep too long, for this I've also learnt –

That if I wake to thick black smoke,
it's well and truly burnt!

MARCH

Our group's known for miles around
  For our very special sound.

Haven't got much expertise:
  Often we're in different keys.

(Paul can only play in F.)

Luckily, we're all tone-deaf.

APRIL

From time to time I feel the urge
                to take a pan and broom
And mop and feather duster,
                and attempt to clean my room.
I empty all the cupboards out
                because I always say
I need to know the things to keep
                and what to throw away.

I spread the stuff across the floor,
                or pile it on the bed:
Those games and toys and t-shirts,
                and those books I've never read.
For hours on end I sort it through,
                without the least success –

For every time I tidy up I make a bigger mess.

MAY

I'm always getting insect bites
    and bruises on the knee;
And grazes on my elbows
    when I climb my favourite tree.

But I can't complain about it
    when I look around and see –

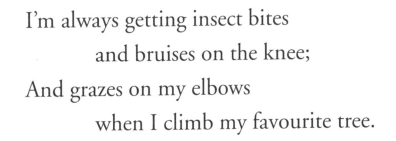

All those many, many others
who are far worse off than me.

JUNE

Our friends are keen on keeping pets;
　　　　　　　　to visit them's a treat.
We watch the creatures groom and climb
　　　　　　　　and stretch and drink and eat.
They romp around the room, they yawn,
　　　　　　　　they doze – all rolled-up tight –
They twitter, squeal, and growl, and purr –

But, most of all, they bite!

JULY

The sun shining brightly; the shade of a tree.
Just right for a picnic, I think you'll agree.
We whoop with delight as the tablecloth's laid:
We all love the cakes and the cool orangeade,
The eggs and the ham and the pickles and cheese.

And so do the ants and the wasps and the bees!

AUGUST

I found a super bathing-place, concealed among the trees.
In Spring it looks delightful – but the water's fit to freeze.
I use it most in August (there's just me and several sheep)
The water's warm and tempting –

But it's only ankle-deep.

SEPTEMBER

My sister's really hopeless
  when she does her magic show.
She thinks she's reached perfection,
  but she's quite a way to go!

The coin will never reappear
  from underneath the cup;
The strings of flags she pulls
  from sleeves are always tangled up;

The mice she tries to conjure up
  from hats are never there –
They're always running round the room,
  or climbing up your chair.
Her clumsiness at card tricks
  ought to cover her with shame;

But we applaud her dazzling skill at juggling, all the same.

OCTOBER

It's funny how different you look in a cape;
Or stuffed with plump cushions to alter your shape;
Or sporting a jerkin; or top-hat and beard.
Except for my brother –

He always looks weird.

NOVEMBER

It's cold outside, but warm indoors, and we have all we need –
We pile up on the sofa and we settle down to read.
What's it to be? Some wizardry? Or medieval knights?
Or something about ponies? Or interstellar flights?
A wild romantic tale for me, a beast in space for Jim,

While Andy hugs a picture book that's twice as big as him.

DECEMBER

Do not disturb.
Don't knock or ring.
I'm staying here –

Until it's SPRING!